Frog Books: The Amazing Frog Book for Kids

101+ Frog Facts, Photos, Quiz and BONUS Word Search Puzzle

Jenny Kellett

ISBN-13: 978-1548639136
ISBN-10: 1548639133

Email: me@jennykellett.com

Printed in U.S.A

Introduction

It's hard not to love frogs! But how much do you really know about your favorite cold-blooded animal?

In this book you will learn over 100 amazing new things about frogs — from Poison Darts to Green frogs. You'll be a frog expert in no time.

Are you ready? Let's go!

Green frog

Frog Facts

Frogs don't need to drink because they absorb water through their skin.

• • •

Frogs are tailless amphibians.

• • •

Most frogs have a simple diet of small insects such as earthworms and spiders. Larger species of frogs may also eat birds, mice and snakes.

Blue poison dart frog

Frogs usually sit and wait for their prey to come near them before capturing it with their long sticky tongues.

• • •

There are three types of amphibians: anura (frogs and toads), caudate (salamanders and newts) and caecilians (worm-like amphibians).

• • •

Frogs can lay up to 4,000 eggs in one sitting.

• • •

Brown frog

Common Chinese tree frog

Frogs have big round ear drums on the side of their heads, which are called tympanum.

• • •

Frogs are color blind; they can only see

in black and white.

• • •

Frogs eyes come in all sorts of shapes and sizes, including heart-shaped and square pupils.

• • •

Frogs range in size from 1cm to 30cm in length.

• • •

Frogs eyes and nose are on top of their heads so that they can breathe and see when the rest of their body is underwater.

Frogs are able to change the color of their skin depending on their environment.

• • •

Frogs can live just as well in water and on land.

• • •

Just like trees, frogs bones develop rings as they age so that scientists are able to determine their age.

• • •

Froglets — or young frogs — have tails,

while adult frogs do not.

• • •

Darwin's frog lives in the cool forest streams of South America. Female Darwin's frogs lay eggs, then the males look after them for about two weeks before carrying the developing young in their throats. When they are small froglets, they simply jump out and swim away.

• • •

Goliath frogs are on the endangered list. They are fast losing their habitat due to ranchers and farmers.

Hunters used to use the poison from Poison Dart frogs to put on the tips of their arrows.

• • •

The North American Wood frog is one of very few species that can live above the Arctic Circle.

• • •

Most frogs can't live in salt water. However, the Florida leopard frog can live in nearly completely salty water.

• • •

Glass frog

Most brightly colored frogs are colored this way to warn predators that they are poisonous.

• • •

Frogs live on every continent except Antarctica.

• • •

Do you know the difference between frogs and toads? Well, actually there aren't any differences. They are the same animal with a different name. However, toads generally refer to the species that have rough skin, while frogs have moist smooth skin.

European Common frog

Golden poison frog

Not all frogs' feet are the same. The shape of their feet depends on the habitat they live in. Frogs that spend most their time in water have webbed feet, while Tree frogs have sticky pads on their toes to help them climb more easily.

• • •

All frogs have four front digits and five back digits on their feet.

• • •

There are more than 5,000 species of frogs in the world, but only 45 species can be found in Europe.

Some frogs can jump over 20 times their own body length.

• • •

Every frog species has its own unique call, some of which can be heard up to a mile away.

• • •

Some frogs, including the Southern Leopard frog, have developed clever stripes on their backs that confuse predators from above by making them look like they aren't frogs.

• • •

Green frog

Asian Tree frogs build their nests in trees above the water so that when their tadpoles hatch they fall directly into the water.

• • •

In some species of frogs, it is only the male that sings. Most frog species have male and female calls.

• • •

Large frogs have deep voices, meaning their calls are at a low frequency. It is the opposite for small frogs, which have loud high-pitched chirps.

Green tree frog

Frogs sing for many reasons, including trying to attract a mate, marking their territory, because they know the weather is going to change (yes, really!) and when they are frightened or hurt.

• • •

What noise do frogs make in your country? Ribbit? Croak? Well, it's different all around the world! For example, in Japan it is 'kerokero' and in Sweden, it's 'kvack'.

• • •

Scientists recently found a painkiller that is 200x as strong as morphine in the

Italian tree frog with an inflamed vocal sac.

Lemur leaf frog

skin of a frog.

• • •

Frog eggs are also known as frog spawn.

• • •

Tadpoles consist of just a tail and gills.

• • •

Very little is known about how long frogs live for in the wild, and it varies between different species. In captivity, though, frogs can live for a very long time -- between 4 and 15 years!

Do you know what the largest enemy is to frogs? It is pollution! However, they also have many natural predators including snakes, lizards, birds and other small animals.

• • •

Some frogs will actually eat smaller frogs.

• • •

The golden dart frog is the most poisonous frog in the world. The skin of one frog can kill up to 1,000 people.

• • •

New England tree frog

Frogs completely shed their skin about once a week. The frog will generally eat it's skin afterwards.

• • •

When a frog swallows its prey, it blinks, which then pushes its eyeballs down on top of the mouth to help push the food down its throat.

• • •

The wood frog, which lives in North America, freezes in winter and then comes back to life when the weather is warmer.

Orange thighed frog

A group of frogs is called an army.

. . .

The Glass frog has translucent skin so you can see all of its internal organs. You can even see its stomach digesting food.

. . .

The Coqui frog is one of the world's loudest. It's voice can reach up to a hundred decibels — that's as loud as a lawnmower.

. . .

Most frogs have teeth, however, they

Panamanian golden frog

are usually only in the upper jaw.

• • •

The Goliath frog is the largest in the world. It lives in West Africa and can grow to the size of a newborn baby.

• • •

The Waxy Monkey frog secretes a wax from its neck, which it rubs over itself with its legs. It uses that wax to prevent its skin from drying out in the sun.

• • •

There is a frog in Indonesia that has no lungs. Instead, it breathes through its skin.

• • •

There is only one frog species that
actually goes 'ribbit'. The reason
Americans, and many other people in
the world, believe that frogs say 'ribbit'
is because when early Hollywood films
were made they would record the sound
of the nearest frog. The species that
lives in that area that goes 'ribbit'!

• • •

Some species of frogs, such as the
Barred Leaf frog, have bright colors
on their legs and underparts that flash

Phantasmal poison frog

when they move to confuse predators.

• • •

The Chilean four-eyed frog has two markings on its back that look like extra eyes. In fact, they are poisonous glands that the frog will show to predators if it feels threatened.

• • •

Albino frogs are not uncommon. So if you see a ghostly looking frog with red eyes, don't worry it's not sick!

• • •

Frogs can use their eyes to help push

food down! They push their eyes deep into their sockets.

• • •

Some people believe that you can get warts from touching a frog or toad, but this is not true!

• • •

Horned frogs have a flap of skin above each eyes that makes it look like they have spiky horns.

• • •

The Catholic frog, which lives in

Red-eyed tree frog

Southern Brown tree frog

Australia, was given its name because of the cross-like pattern on its back.

• • •

The Flat-headed frog, which also lives in Australia, protects itself in the dry climate by storing up lots of water in its body so it appears to be very round and bloated.

• • •

The most common frogs found above the Arctic Circle are Wood frogs. This species hibernate during the winter by burrowing beneath the ground to prevent themselves from freezing to death. The first thing they do when they wake up is go look for a mating partner.

• • •

The earliest frogs lived around 190 million years ago during the late Jurassic period. Scientists believe that frogs developed their ability to jump to escape from dinosaurs.

• • •

Fossils of the earliest known frogs have been found on Navajo Indian reservations in Arizona.

• • •

Strawberry poison frog

Tree frog

The smallest frog in the Southern Hemisphere is the Gold frog. They grow to just 9.8mm in length!

. . .

The smallest frog in the Northern Hemisphere was discovered so recently that it hasn't been given a common name yet, but it's scientific name is but its scientific name is Eleutherodactylus iberia.

. . .

A fear of frogs is called ranidaphobia and a fear of all amphibians is called batrachophobia. But we guess you don't have either of those!

Many cultures believe that frogs are associated with weather. Native Americans and Australian Aborigines believed that frogs were the bringer of rain. Whereas in India, frogs are believed to mean that thunder is coming.

• • •

In China, they don't see the 'man in the moon' they see the toad in the moon!

• • •

In Japan, frogs are the symbol for good luck.

Waxy monkey leaf frog

Throughout history there have been many stories of it 'raining frogs', but it turns out it actually happens! These frog storms happen when gusts of strong wind pick up small frogs from a pond and then drop them elsewhere.

• • •

A group of frogs is called an army of frogs.

• • •

A group of toads is called a knot of toads.

• • •

Frogs are able to look forwards, behinds and to the sides without needing to turn their heads!

• • •

Tadpoles breathe through their gills.

• • •

Scientists are studying frogs to see if they can help sick people get better.

• • •

The study of frogs (and other amphibians) is called herpetology.

In July 2017, a study found that frogs may have been partly to blame for the extinction of the dinosaurs. After the extinction, the population of frogs exploded.

. . .

Frogs are very important for preventing diseases in humans. They help to control populations of potential disease-carrying insects, such as in areas along the River Nile.

. . .

Frogs sit in the middle of the food chain, so they are a very important part of our earth's ecosystem.

• • •

Frogs were the first land animals with
vocal chords.

• • •

The Costa Rican Flying Tree frog can
leap long distances between trees thanks
to its webbed feet that help it to glide.

• • •

The Gastric Brooding frog, which lives in
Australia, swallows her fertilised eggs.
When they are ready to be born, they
hop out of her mouth.

Frog Quiz

Now test your knowledge in the Frog Quiz! Answers can be found on page 57.

1. Frogs belong to a group of animals called what?

2. Where do frogs spend their lives living?

3. Are frogs cold-blooded or warm-blooded?

4. What part of their body do frogs use to help them swallow?

White-lipped tree frog

5. Frogs are found on every continent except...?

6. Which way can a frog look without turning its head?

7. Frogs can lay up to how many eggs?

8. Tadpoles breathe using their...?

9. Adult frogs breathe using their...?

10. The Red Eyed tree frog sleeps with its eyes open. True or false?

11. What substance is on a Tree frog's toes to help them climb trees?

12. All frogs use their tongues to catch prey. True or false?

13. How do most frogs drink water?

14. What are frog eggs also known as?

15. What do tadpoles consist of?

16. What is the difference between a froglet and a frog?

Australian Green Tree frog

Answers:

1. Amphibians
2. Both in water and on land
3. Cold-blooded, like all amphibians
4. Eyes
5. Antarctica
6. Forwards, behinds and to the side
7. 20,000
8. Gills
9. Lungs and skin
10. Closed. It opens its eyes if it gets startled.
11. A sticky mucus.
12. False. The African clawed frog has no tongue.
13. It is absorbed through their skin.
14. Frog spawn
15. A tail and gills.
16. A froglet has a tail and a frog does not.

FROGS
WORDSEARCH

W	F	G	F	S	P	A	W	N	T	R	E
Q	Y	B	D	S	A	S	D	F	A	V	G
A	T	N	A	S	D	P	Y	D	M	D	O
S	R	T	R	E	E	D	H	S	P	S	L
D	E	F	A	Z	F	Z	E	R	H	A	I
F	S	D	S	D	C	F	W	E	I	S	A
A	R	M	Y	F	P	R	A	W	B	E	T
B	F	F	E	D	F	O	S	S	I	D	H
F	D	Q	B	W	D	G	L	D	A	D	D
F	R	O	G	A	D	L	D	E	N	F	A
S	S	F	D	S	A	E	V	D	S	A	D
D	S	G	F	D	A	T	O	A	D	D	S

Can you find all the words below in the wordsearch puzzle on the left?

TADPOLE   GOLIATH   TOAD

FROGLET   TREE   AMPHIBIAN

FROG   SPAWN   ARMY

We hope you learnt some awesome facts about frogs!

Follow Bellanova Books on Facebook for the latest book releases and special offers.

Printed in Great Britain
by Amazon